SIMON AND SCHUSTER

SIMON AND SCHUSTER
First published in Great Britain in 2013 by Simon and Schuster UK Ltd
1st Floor, 222 Gray's Inn Road, London WC1X 8HB
A CBS Company

Based on the television series Mike the Knight
© 2012 HIT (MTK) Limited/Nelvana Limited. A United Kingdom-Canada Co-production.

ISBN 978-1-4711-1591-2

Printed and bound in China
10 9 8 7 6 5 4 3 2 1
www.simonandschuster.co.uk

Mike THE KNIGHT

and the Real Sword

It's time for Mike to have
his portrait done,
but without a real sword,
it doesn't seem much fun.
With whatever you have,
you can do quite a lot
and a true knight will just
use whatever he's got!

Great knights have their portrait painted by a
Royal Painter.

Mike the Knight was practising his poses. "Sparkie!
Squirt! I need a really knightly pose for the
painting. What do you think of this?"

"Yip! Yap! No!" Queen Martha called. The pups were running around and they tripped up the Royal Painter!

"Maybe I should take them for a walk to calm them down, Mum," Evie said.

Queen Martha agreed. "But don't go too far. I don't want them to get dirty."

While the Royal Painter cleaned himself up, Mike, Sparkie and Squirt went to check Mike's Big Book for Little Knights-in-Training for a knightly pose.

Mike saw a picture of a knight holding up his sword. "That pose is really knightly!

By the King's crown, that's it!

I'm Mike the Knight and my mission is to look really knightly for the royal painting!"

Mike drew his enchanted sword to pose like the picture. "Aw! A fishing rod? I'm tired of waiting for Evie's spell to wear off. Let's go and find her!"

Mike pulled the secret lever to put on his armour.

Now ready for action,
Mike found Evie walking Yip and Yap.
"Evie! You have to turn my sword back or I'm
never going to look knightly in the royal painting!"
"Hmm," Evie thought. "I could try this spell…"

Evie looked at Yip and Yap. "You two sit on that tree stump. I don't want you getting dirty."

She raised her wand and read out of her book:
"Begone, vamoose - I'll say it clear:
Magic, take away what's here!"

"Oh!" Mike grumbled. "It's still a fishing rod! Your magic didn't do anything!"

It was strangely quiet.

"Mike!" Evie cried. "Yip and Yap are gone! My magic did do something!"

"I think I hear them!" Mike said. "They're in the woods. Come on!"

Mike and Galahad charged ahead, while Evie and Mr Cuddles took her scooter, with Sparkie and Squirt following behind them.

The young knight found Yip and Yap stranded in the middle of a muddy puddle.

"Oh no!" Evie shook her head. "Mum told me to make sure they stayed clean!"

"Don't worry, Evie," Mike said. "I'll rescue them."

Mike and Galahad fetched the trebuchet. "I'm going to fire myself across the mud – over to Yip and Yap!"

"Wouldn't it be easier to use the fishing rod to lift them out?" Evie suggested.

"No," Mike said. "That wouldn't be very knightly."

"Mike!" said Sparkie. "I've found this stick for you. It looks just like a real sword. You can use it for the portrait."

"Thanks, Sparkie!" Mike said and climbed into the basket of the trebuchet. "Okay! Fire me!"

Mike flew high into the air, over the bubbling mud and landed straight on top of…

…the stump next to Yip and Yap!

"Well done, Mike!" Everyone cheered.

But Mike didn't look so happy. "Now I'm stuck in the middle of the mud with Yip and Yap! If only I had a real sword, then I'd chop this tree stump to pieces to make stepping stones."

Mike was really frustrated. "Evie! You have to change this fishing rod into a real sword – please!! Use a better, bigger spell!"

"Okay," Evie said, "I'll try:
Bigger magic, fly, I say
Make that fishing rod go away!"

"Oh! It's still a fishing rod!" Mike frowned. Suddenly, the tree stump started to grow taller and taller.

"I'm sorry, Mike! My magic didn't quite work." Evie quickly searched her book for another spell.

"No, Evie, wait. We're only up here because I kept asking you to magic me a real sword," Mike smiled. **"It's time to be a knight and do it right!**

A real knight doesn't worry about a sword. He just uses whatever he has. And I have a fishing rod and this stick!"

"Sparkie! Hook this line to a tree." Mike cast the fishing line across to Sparkie. Sparkie caught the line and tied it round a nearby tree. Mike made sure the fishing rod was fixed to the tree stump.

Mike took off his helmet and carefully placed Yip and Yap inside. Hooking the helmet over the fishing line, Mike gave the helmet a gentle push. "Enjoy your ride!"

The pups landed safe and sound.

"What about you, Mike?" Evie shouted.

"No problem! Watch!" Mike put Sparkie's sword stick over the fishing line and held on to each end. He slid down over the mud and to the ground. **"Weeee!"**

"Woo-hoo-hoo!" Squirt cheered.
"Wow! Go, Mike!"
Sparkie roared.

"Thanks for the stick sword, Sparkie! But I don't need a sword to look knightly in the painting," Mike said, giving the stick back.

"You don't?" Sparkie asked.

"A knight looks knightly with whatever he's got!" Mike smiled.

HUZZAH!